COELWULF'S COMPANY

Tales from before The Last King

M J Porter

M J Publishing

ISBN (ebook): 978-1-914332-72-2
ISBN (paperback): 978-1-914332-73-9

Cover design by: M J Publishing
Sword design by: Shaun at Flintlock Covers

CONTENTS

INTRODUCTION

C oelwulf's Company is a collection of short stories featuring the characters from The Ninth Century/The Last King series of books. I thought it would be interesting to examine how the group of warriors first came together. There are some hints throughout the books, but to write these events from difference perspectives was too good an opportunity to miss.

This short story collection came about because of my new project, Son of Mercia, with Boldwood Books, the first book in The Eagle of Mercia Chronicles. You won't know this just yet, but fans of The Ninth Century books will, I hope, be delighted to know that this series will be telling the story of Icel as a youngster.

The Last King starts in
AD874. These stories take

place before then.

ICEL

AD864

I can feel her eyes blazing into me, but I refuse to meet them. Instead, my focus stays on the faltering body of my oath-sworn lord, Coenwulf. He's dying. I know it. He knows it. Lady Cyneswith knows it, and yet she refuses to accept it. She's as stubborn as bloody Edmund.

The room is too warm, and sweat slips from Coenwulf's forehead as though rainwater. I sigh. This is not how a man like him should meet his end. Better to have died on the battlefield than here, his wounds rotted by the filth with which the Raiders smeared their weapons. How I detest the Raiders. I've fought them all my life, and still, they attack Mercia. I won't stop defeating them until they realise their cause is hopeless.

How many times must one man kill to keep his kingdom safe?

"Icel," the sharp crack of a broken voice reaches

me, drags me from my musings.

"My Lady," I bow my head. I've known her since she was no taller than my knee, and yet, she is the lady here and always has been.

"You can help him." I shrug my enormous shoulders. I'm helpless. I wish I could. But I can't.

"Those skills have long since left me. I haven't practised them for too long. You, My Lady, know far more than I do. The monks have shared their carefully hoarded knowledge with you, not with me."

Edmund's exasperated sigh reaches my ears. He stands, hand on his seax, and I think him likely to stab me with it. I hold my hands to either side of me. This isn't something that threat and fear can solve. I simply don't know.

"I don't know how," Lady Cyneswith pleads with me.

"And why should I, My Lady? I don't know how to cure, only how to maim." Her eyes flash angrily.

"I know you do have the knowledge, the skills. When I was a girl, you aided anyone you could, even the damn enemy, and now you let your oath lord die?" The fact she says 'damn' assures me she's on edge, almost beyond her endurance. I don't believe she's slept for two days. She watches her nephew die before her eyes, and she's incapable of saving him because he can't be saved.

"If threat won't bring the knowledge to me, I assure you that pleading won't either. I do not know. I only wish I did."

A hand on my shoulder, and now I sigh softly,

stepping clear from Edmund's attempt to threaten me. Another man might find his grip would hold them in place, but it's as nothing to me.

"Don't drive me from his side. I will remain. Until there is nothing to remain for."

"No," Coenwulf shocks me by speaking. The words are surprisingly strong for a man who's not stood for three days. "You'll fetch my brother." There's no anguish in his words, just stubbornness.

"No," Edmund replies immediately.

"No," Lady Cyneswith gasps. "It will not come to that."

"It will, and I know it will. Now, I'm your oath-sworn lord as well. You must do as I command. Icel. Edmund. Fetch my brother. Kingsholm can't be without a lord; without its ealdorman."

I open my mouth and snap it shut again. My mind has fallen down the pit of memories. It holds me, immobile.

Coenwulf and Coelwulf. Did two children ever have such an impact on the life of a man who wasn't their father? I remember it all. Before me, I see the two of them pass through their lives, from squalling babes to cheeky boys, to angry youths. It pains me to know that I've seen it all when their mother didn't. It pains me to know that I'll watch Coenwulf die just as I once did his mother, his father as well.

I would say this household has been cursed, but I don't believe in such. We've lived through dangerous times when to die was the expectation, to live was abnormal.

I open my eyes, try to beat back the images before me, but they don't dissipate. Every inch of this room holds one memory or another, all the way back to the first time I stepped into this hall, with the rain lashing at my back. I didn't know then what my future would hold. I couldn't even have guessed the events that would befall me.

I banish them all, see instead the first steps Coenwulf took, the way his mother watched on, pride on her face, hand on her distended belly. She didn't live to see Coelwulf take his first steps.

Above my head, old and broken shields speak of a triumph missing for decades from Kingsholm. Lord Coenwulf was not frightened of who he was, and I did believe he would reconstruct the family's fortunes, but it wasn't to be. The Raiders had seen to that.

"I'll do it," I confirm to Coenwulf. I'll fulfil his dying wish because we both know that's what it is, and he has my oath, and I must do as he commands. Equally, I would do it anyway if he asked. He has been my friend as well as my lord.

"No," Lady Cyneswith reiterates. "Icel is your only hope to live," she tries to convince Coenwulf.

"There's no more hope, dear aunt. This is where my life will end. I'm wise enough to accept that, even if I wasn't wise enough to stay away from the damn Raiders' blade." Damn is the least of Coenwulf's expletives. It sounds strange to my ears to hear such an innocuous-sounding word, but of course, he speaks so as not to offend his aunt. She's never approved of the vulgarity more likely to pepper our conversations.

"Then you go alone," Edmund announces, armed folded stubbornly over his broad chest.

"Edmund, I'm your oath-sworn lord. You obey me or break that oath, and I'll release you from my household troop." There's no compassion in Coenwulf's voice. He means to be obeyed. Edmund is a bloody fool to think he can deny Coenwulf. How much easier their lives would have been if they'd been the brothers and not Coenwulf and Coelwulf.

"I'll not leave you," he persists, his voice cracking on the words.

"Then I'll have you banned from my presence." Coenwulf hasn't been so lucid for over a day, tossing and turning as the fever took him, as the unhealing wound began to poison him.

"You wouldn't?" There's hurt as well as fear in Edmund's voice. I shake my head. It pains me to see such obstinacy when the outcome is far beyond our abilities to control.

"If you disobey me, then there'll be no choice. If I'm seen faltering, now, while I lie dying, rumours will spread that Kingsholm is weak. Despite her strong walls and her fierce warriors, the Raiders will sniff out the weakness and come for her. I'll not allow that." Coenwulf's words sound louder than thunder. I wince at the bite to them. How Edmund can still doubt Coenwulf's resolve, I don't know, and yet his mouth opens.

"Hold," Coenwulf says. "No more words, only actions. That is how my warriors have always carried themselves, showed their worth to me."

Edmund's jaw snaps shut audibly. I keep my eyes on Coenwulf. I don't need to see the anguished look that passes between Edmund and Lady Cyneswith. I can imagine it well enough.

A smirk touches Coenwulf's lips, a shared moment between us. Perhaps it'll be the last one. That single look says much and nothing.

"You'll help my brother," Coenwulf whispers. I bend to hear him. I shudder at the words, and this time Coenwulf's smirk is filled with scorn.

"He'll become a better man. He is a better man. Brothers don't have to love one another. Sometimes, they're better apart." I don't know if there's any truth to those words. I've never had a brother. Every brotherhood I've known has had its difficulties. Still, I'm curious enough to listen.

"I'll take your word for it," I smirk, placing my hand on his feebly rising chest. He lifts his hand and grips mine.

"Take care of them all, Icel. I beg you." I grunt. This is too much for one man, but when has Coenwulf, or any other of my lords, ever thought to demand less from me?

"I'll do my best. I'll do better than my best," I reiterate. "I'll not let you down."

This seems to satisfy Coenwulf, and he releases my hand. I stand once more. The moment between Edmund and Lady Cyneswith has passed. Now both of them stand aloof, neither liking what's going to happen next.

I survey the hall before me. Coenwulf has refused to lie in the ruins of the monks' infirmary, determined to remain at the centre of Kingsholm. His warriors sit and talk in muted tones, every so often casting a baleful look in the direction of their oath-sworn lord. Some, I imagine, already suspect that Coenwulf will not recover from his wound. Amongst their number, I include Pybba and Hereman, Edmund's brother. Also Cenred. He's seen enough wounds in his life to know what can and can't be healed.

But of the younger men, many of them will not accept the sign that their lord isn't inexorable. When we next ride to war, which we will, and probably quite soon, they'll be wary. Their movements will not be as smooth as usual. They'll doubt their abilities. For that reason, it'll be best if our new lord is quick to anger and ride out against the Raiders, or the men of Wessex, whichever it is that tries to attack when news of Coenwulf's death leaks beyond the walls of Kingsholm.

"Well, get going," Coenwulf wheezes. I meet his eyes. They're pain-hazed but determined.

"You must give him something for the pain," I inform Lady Cyneswith, but I don't wait for her answer. Time is pressing, and I need to ready my horse. If I move first, Edmund will have no choice but to follow me.

"What's happening?" Pybba rushes to walk beside me, opening the door into the interior of the residential complex

"He is dying," there's no compassion in my words. "He demands I retrieve his brother, although where I'm to find him, I don't know."

I hear Pybba suck in a harsh breath as we walk onto the wooden floorboards of the stable floor.

"He can be found in Hereford at this time," Pybba informs me, no hint of apology in his words.

I open my mouth and close it once more.

Pybba raises his eyebrows as though expecting some argument and prepared to ward against it.

"My thanks," I astonish him by saying.

"Aye, you must travel safely and quickly."

"Will we need an additional horse?" I ask next, determined to test the extent of Pybba's knowledge.

"No, he has that brute, Haden."

A smile plays around my lips at that news.

"He can run from Kingsholm, but he can't run from Haden."

At the sound of the other horse's name, a piebald nose appears over the stable. I meet Dever's eyes with pity. Dever is Coenwulf's horse. He'll never be ridden by his master again. What will happen to him now, I don't know? Pybba reaches across the divide and rubs his gnarled hand over the black and white nose, finding something for Dever to snaffle as well.

Dever and Haden, two horses who were brothers themselves and ridden by two brothers. They shared a sire, but little else other than that. Dever is the older, the more placid. Haden is the younger, the quicker to anger, the quicker to bite and kick and snarl if a horse can be said to do such a thing.

It's growing late outside. We'll ride during the darkness, but we can't wait for the sunrise the following morning. It might be too late if we do so. Samson obediently allows me to saddle him, to ensure his saddle fits firmly. And still, Edmund doesn't follow me.

I sigh, tying the reins to a hook on the wall, and walking to Jethson's stable. Jethson is not a placid beast. I expect some outrage from him, but he allows me into his stable without doing anything untoward. Only then does he stamp on my foot or try to. I force him away from me.

"Easy now," I instruct him. Pybba is there, with the saddle and the reins. Between us, we manage to saddle him, despite his backward steps and evasions. Even so, in such a small space, I'm impressed by how much he manages to slow our progress.

Pybba tries to calm him with wizened apples and even a purple carrot, but while Jethson takes them eagerly enough, they don't calm him down.

"Leave him." Edmund's voice is furious. I turn to meet his angry eyes.

"Then hurry the fuck up," I retort. "I don't want to chase down Coelwulf, but if I must, then I want it done sooner rather than later. There's no point if we return to find Coenwulf already dead."

I think Edmund will reply, but he bends his head and continues saddling Jethson. The two of them make a fine pair, brooding and challenging to manage.

"What are you doing?" Hereman has arrived, filled with questions.

"What's it got to do with you?" Edmund's rage is directed squarely at Hereman. Hereman looks to Pybba and me. Two brothers, so often at loggerheads.

"We go to find Coelwulf. He must return and take his brother's place." Hereman stills. He's a tall man, always moving, always doing something without thought, but for once, he considers what he's been told before answering.

I watch him heavily swallow before he speaks.

"Do you need company? The Raiders are still out there?"

"No, we'll go quickly, and just the two of us. Remain here. You and Pybba will have command while we're gone. Emit no one. Allow no one to leave, not even the monks or the priest. While our lord's force is split, it can't be divided any further."

Hereman nods. I'm impressed by his resolution. Edmund doesn't speak to him but leads Jethson to the stables' exterior, ready to mount up. Hereman goes with him.

"I'm sorry," we all hear his words. There's nothing for Hereman to be sorry for, but it's rather an expression of the anguish he appreciates his brother must be feeling.

"Fuck off," Edmund rewards his brother's compassion with none of his own. Hereman steps from his brother's side, eyes on the ground. Edmund should be pleased he's still standing. If another had spoken like that, he'd be sitting on his arse, his head ringing, wondering which way's up and which way's down.

"Good luck with him," Hereman turns to me, eyes blazing with anger. "Edmund's a fucking arse. Make sure our new lord understands that." I startle at the words, but Hereman is unrepentant.

"It's about time we had someone who'll kick him up the arse and tell him what's what."

I'm stunned into silence, Pybba as well, and then Hereman begins to laugh, the sound hardly cheering.

"Don't tell me that's not what concerns you?" He spits at his brother. "When we have a new lord, he'll think nothing of you, and for once, I might fucking win our fights." So spoken, Hereman turns aside, without speaking further to his brother, and I mount Samson without looking at Edmund.

Nothing else needs saying. Hereman is no doubt correct in his summary, but that doesn't concern me. I have My Lord's last wishes to carry out, and I mean to do so.

COELWULF

AD864

I eye the man before me with undisguised loathing. Edmund, with his flashing green eyes and
smart byrnie and weapons belt. He wears more
wealth around his body than I could ever hope to
own.

"What do you fucking want?" I don't like him. I
never have.

Now he sighs, heavily, using his right hand to
brush the mass of hair away from his forehead and
eyes. No doubt he doesn't like it to get in the way.
How then will the swooning women know him for
a good looking man? Because even I can recognise
someone who's pleasing to the opposite sex, my own
as well.

"You need to come with me," Edmund informs
me, his words snapped and sharp.

"Why the fuck do I need to do that?" I won't return
to Kingsholm. I hate that place. It stinks of failure,

and not just mine.

"Your brother is dying. He wishes to speak with you."

I blink, swallow, unsure how I'm supposed to feel about that, but Edmund is already hauling me up by my left arm, another man I don't much like beside him, taking the right. Icel. He's a bastard as well.

"What do you mean he's dying? Why hasn't my Aunt saved him?"

The words tumble from me as the pair of them pull me clear from my place on the wooden bench where I've been warming my arse. It's not cold outside. It's nearly the height of summer, but I've managed to get close enough to the hearth, and I'm not about to give it up, even if I'm sweating.

I chuckle on seeing that Icel tries not to breathe too deeply. I'm sure I stink as well. But, I've done a fair day's labour for a fair wage, and I don't see that's anything about which to be ashamed.

"No," the word is hard, once more, edged with more than just denial.

I turn to gaze at Icel. He's a giant of a man. A nasty bastard if ever I saw one. When I was younger, he had black hair and a beard that aroused jealously in every man. Now, he's greying but no less fierce. I can't even consider how old he is. Not as old as my dead father would have been. Or perhaps he is. How the fuck would I know?

"Coelwulf," Icel dips his head to me, something in his eyes alerting me to the fact that this isn't easy for him.

"What's he dying from?" I try not to slur my words. I've drunk my body weight in ale that night. It tasted like shit, but it brought oblivion until now.

"The wound-rot." I wince to hear that. It's not a good way to go.

"From what wound?" Abruptly, Edmund comes to a stop, and my body's held uncomfortably tight as Icel moves on.

"Shut the fuck up, and we'll tell you everything you need to know." I nod, swallow down the nausea pooling in my throat and sour stomach. I don't like the sound of this.

Edmund eyes me, and again I'm struck by the unusual shade of his eyes. A man such as him shouldn't have been given quite so many gifts by his mother and father. Rumour, if I ever listened to it, tells me that he's left a trail of broken hearts in his wake. Lucky fucker. I've never had much luck with the opposite sex. Perhaps it might be different if I didn't stink and wallow in my own self-pity. But, fuck, that's too much trouble for me.

And then he speaks as he and Icel continue to direct my steps. I'd like to say I don't need their support. That would be a bloody lie.

"Lord Coenwulf." Hearing my brother's name makes it all seem too real. Damn the bastard. Why is he dying?

"Was wounded by a Raider. They fouled the blade, and now the wound won't heal, and more, poisons him. Lady Cyneswith is unable to do more for him. He's weak and will die soon. He's been asking for you in his fever."

Edmund speaks calmly, but I can hear the rage behind those words. I consider just what it's taken for him to leave Kingsholm and seek me out, here, in some half-forsaken tavern in Hereford. This close to the border, I can be assured of a fight with someone whenever I fancy it. And I desire it quite a lot.

"How did you find me?" I think to ask, even as they lever me over my horse's back. How the fuck did they know where my horse was?

I think they might tie me in the saddle. The reputation of my horse is fiercer than mine.

"Can you ride?" Icel demands. His words rumble loudly, startling the other animals in the stable as I hear hooves kicking wooden doors.

"Yes, if you keep bloody Jethson away from Haden."

"Ah, yes. I'd forgotten," and Icel inserts himself between Edmund's mount and mine. The two horses have never liked each other, not even when they were mere colts. Now they're as old and wise as I am, and still, they hate one another. You've got to admire that sort of persistence. I chuckle to myself. After all these years apart, I could be forgiven for thinking that one of them, or both of them, might finally have let it go. But no.

I duck my head below the door of the stables, rifling in my saddle bag for a coin for the lad who waits there, disappointment on his face that Haden is leaving.

"Here," and I throw him something. It flashes beneath the flames of the brazier and the lad's eyes alight and then glow ever brighter.

"A silver penny for looking after your horse? What was he doing with him?" Icel asks in a low murmur of wonder. I shake my head. I hadn't meant to gift that particular coin. But, I'm not the sort of man to ask for it back. The little shit could eat well for some time off that coin, provided he gets to keep it.

"Pybba knew where you were. It seems the bishop's been keeping an eye on you," Edmund eventually announces, pulling his cloak around his face to shield it from the light rain that's begun to fall.

"And why would that be?" I feel aggrieved. I just want to be treated like any other has-been.

"I don't know. Pybba told me. No doubt your aunt made some agreement with the man."

That makes me shut my mouth. My Aunt. Was there ever a more terrifying woman on this earth?

"Can he gallop?" Edmund eyes Haden with undisguised loathing.

"Of course he bloody can," I'm stung into replying.

"Good. We need to hurry, or we'll be too late," the bleakness of the response stops me from making any further comment. Edmund has been my brother's warrior for at least the last decade. They're closer than Coenwulf, and I have ever been. Edmund will grieve for my brother more than I will. We've not exactly been friends, my brother and I, merely family.

Icel rides silently in front of me, Haden picking

his hooves up to ensure he stays at the same pace, and every single movement jostles my head until I can barely keep my eyes open.

"We need to stop," I call. My tongue feels too large in my mouth, and my belly churns. Any moment now, and I'm going to lose all that fine ale. Well, not fine ale. Shit ale. I'm going to lose all that shit ale.

"There isn't time," Edmund huffs even as I slow Haden, bringing him to a canter and then a trot. Close by, I can hear a stream.

"I need to drink something."

"Then have water," Icel snarls, pointing towards the water. I'd sooner have more ale, but perhaps water will do as well to drive away my raging thirst.

"Fine," and I attempt to dismount, only to lose my footing in the darkness and land on my arse amid a puddle.

"Fucking marvellous." I stagger to my feet, not bothering to dry my hands, wet from the grasses on the roadway. I've landed on a great big thistle or nettle, knowing my luck. That'll make itself known soon enough.

There's little light from the moon, thanks to the scudding rain clouds, but the water is easy enough to hear, and eagerly, I stumble to my knees to scoop the fluid into my parched mouth. The coldness hitting my throat snaps me fully awake. And still, I drink.

Coenwulf. Dying? It doesn't seem possible. My brother, the ealdorman of the Hwicce, has always been a mighty warrior and somehow able to stomach the ineffectual King Burgred and his sickening alliance with the kingdom of Wessex. I'd have happily killed the bastard myself. Better to have taken myself away when it became clear I wasn't cut out for the life of an ealdorman's brother.

But still, what does it mean for me now that he's dying? And now fear takes me. I stand, turn to Edmund, where he remains mounted, although Jethson has been allowed to pull at the grasses on the road while Icel holds Haden's reins.

"What does my brother expect me to do?" I shout the words. They ring with my fear. I don't fucking like it. Not at all.

Edmund shakes his head.

"I know nothing about that. All I know is that he wanted to see his younger brother before he died."

"And that's all he wanted?"

"Yes," Icel's single word response doesn't allow any further argument. I stagger back to Haden, mount up, and we continue our gallop, the light steadily growing as we come ever closer to Kingsholm, but my thoughts are clear now.

My brother might hope to see me before he dies, but what if he wants something else from me? He has no son, no one to leave Kingsholm to, other than me. And I sure as shit don't want it. I can't help thinking this is all a trick and one from which I've no chance of escaping. If I turned Haden's head now and tried to make my way back to Hereford, Edmund and Icel would hunt me down.

I swallow uneasily. They're not the mild-man-

nered men who help my brother in running the
ealdordom. No, they're killers, both of them, vicious
and nasty bastards who'll kill a Raider, a Wessex
man, and rumour has it, any Welshman before asking his name. I'm not unskilled with a weapon. I
know some would even call me quite good, but I'd be
nothing against these two bastards.

Eyes alert to everything around me, I ride on, oc-
casionally offering some encouragement to Haden.
He's not used to riding such long distances, and I'd
ask for the pace to slow, but Haden wouldn't thank
me for that.

We clatter over the decrepit wooden bridge at
Kempsey, and now I want to slow our headlong
dash as well because as the world starts to come
into focus, the murk of the River Severn, the brightness of the budding flowers and crop-fields, I realise
something. I'll see my brother today, and it'll be for
the last time. All the ways I've imagined this meeting will be as nothing. And, I won't be able to tell him
what I think of his piss-poor attempts to keep Kingsholm free from Mercia's enemies.

Unbidden, a single tear falls down my cheek, and
I scuff it aside, noting my filthy nails as I do so. I
spent yesterday in the fields harvesting the summer
crops. It's not like I had anything better to do, and it
paid me, if not much. Today is going to be entirely
different.

Edmund doesn't slow our speed even as the gate-
way to Kingsholm rushes up before me, the famil-

iar wooden structure surrounding what used to be a king's palace, but hasn't been for many years. I glance upwards, noting the men on watch there. They must have been waiting for Edmund.

I catch a fleeting glance of Pybba, Hereman, Tatberht, Eoppa, Ælfgar, Cuthwalh, Eadfrith, Osmod, Cealwin, Athelstan and Beornberht as well, men I've known for many years, but who are my brother's warriors. And then we're inside the gates, and they're being closed behind us. For a moment, I consider escape, but I take too long.

"Does he yet live?" I find Icel's cry callous and consider telling him as much as I take in the hive of industry before me in the place where I spent my childhood.

"For now," the voice that answers is whip-sharp, and unconsciously, I sit straighter in my saddle, hold my body tight, even though I want to sag with exhaustion after a long night of riding.

"Hurry up," Edmund's words are flung over his shoulder as he surges towards the main hall. I want to linger, take my time before facing this inevitable moment. I'm not going to get my wish.

"Coelwulf, your brother needs you." My Aunt's words are as sharp as Edmund's, if not sharper. I disappoint her. I always have. I glance at her. She hasn't changed. She hasn't even aged, and she still terrifies me.

With no eagerness but some hurry, I swing my leg over Haden's back, noting as I do that my arse does indeed sting from whatever I fell on during the ride.

Wonderful.

"I'll take him," a very young face looks up at me, skinny wrist extended towards me to take Haden's reins.

"I think someone stronger," I try and counter. Haden can be a bastard when he wants to be. He'd have this lad on his arse, or over his back, in no time.

"There's no one else," the boy suggests, looking around him. So much for a grand welcome. Anyone who witnessed my arrival has disappeared. Even Icel leads his horse, Brimman, to the stables. But the lad can only be about five, maybe six at a push. He doesn't even reach Haden's nose.

"Be careful with him," I sigh uneasily. The lad seems bright enough, but, well, it's Haden. He's far too young to have ever seen Haden before.

"What's his name? I'm Rudolf."

"Haden," I inform him, wishing there was some-one else or even that I could just leave my horse here, alone, until I can return to him.

"Come on, horsey," the voice is high and soft. "Haden, you're a good boy, aren't you?" the lad con-tinues to coax, and fuck me, the bastard bends his head low, whiffling the boy's thick head of hair, and allows himself to be led away. I watch with my jaw on the ground. I've never seen another master my mount in such a way.

I stand, feeling the ground beneath my feet, the ache in my legs, the stinging of my arse, and then I pull my tunic down, ensure my weapons belt is in place, and stride towards the main hall.

Inside, it's well lit, a hearth blazing fiercely and over which several cooking pots are suspended. I glance upwards, noting the shields that line the higher arches of the wooden hall. They're in various stages of decay, although two of them are brightly pained with Mercia's twin-headed eagle.

A few people note my passing, but no one speaks to me. I only see bowed heads. Ahead, there's a collection of men and women, Edmund amongst them, my Aunt as well. I hurry my steps to stand beside them.

I'm really not the person to summon when someone lies dying. Even if they are my brother.

And then I hear a feeble voice, querulously demanding water. I'd know that voice anywhere, but I'm shocked by it. My brother has never spoken in anything other than a roar.

The crowd parts to let me closer, and I sag to my knees, noting my nettle sting once more when my arse touches the back of my knees.

"He's here, My Lord," Edmund announces with all the enthusiasm of a man finding horse shit on his boots.

"Good, leave us," the words, softly spoken, are immediately obeyed.

And then we're alone, and I meet my brother's eyes, horrified by the weakness there. His face is whiter than snow, his skin threaded with blue veins that seem to bulge, and when he reaches for my hand, I can see where it shakes.

But his first words are unexpected.

"You fucking stink," he announces, hardly the welcome I was expecting.

"A man sometimes has to labour for a living."

"Calling yourself a man now, are you?" Instead, I bite back my anger and find a smile on my lips. Even now, my brother will bicker with me. I admire him.

"Aye." I lapse into silence.

"I'm dying," Coenwulf informs me. There's no tremor in his voice, just acceptance.

"Edmund said as much."

"With his usual tact?" Coenwulf's lips turn up slightly as he speaks.

"Always."

"You know what this means for you, don't you?" I'm already shaking my head to deny those words.

"Believe me, if there were an alternative, I would have found it by now," Coenwulf advises me with a hint of apology in his words.

"You'll be the ealdorman on my death. You'll be the leader of my warriors."

I choke at that statement.

"You expect Edmund to take orders from me?" There's a squeak of protest in my words.

"Well, you either make him obey you, or you'll be taking orders from him. I can tell you which is easier on your ears, but it's not what I'd choose."

"Can we not just let it go?" And now Coenwulf's grip is fierce.

"Our father wasn't the man he should have been. I don't deny that. But it's our birthright, and you can't walk away from it." I think I can do precisely that.

"You can't," Coenwulf announces. "Even if you want to. What would happen to our Aunt?" I find my eyes seeking her out. She's busy with some tasks, undoubtedly preparing more herbs for my brother. She's highly skilled at healing. It surprises me that Icel speaks with her; the two heads bent so close together it could be inappropriate if I didn't know better.

I think my Aunt would make a far better ealdorman than I would. I think my brother does as well. Indeed, if she'd been born a man, I wouldn't be here. There'd be no need.

"You'll take my position and my warriors. Swear to me." I shake my head. This is too much. Far too much.

"Swear it," Coenwulf demands, his voice a growl, and fuck me, but I do.

"I swear it, on my life."

A silence forms between us, and then Coenwulf coughs heavily, his chest heaving. Only when he's recovered does he look at me, his familiar eyes filled with sorrow and understanding.

"Thank fuck you didn't swear it on my life."

EDMUND

AD864

I eye him. I hate him. Why he lives when my lord is dead, I don't understand. And now? Now Coenwulf expects me to serve his brother? I don't fucking think so.

I've bowed my head over Coenwulf's grave inside Kingsholm, in the churchyard. I've made the sounds that I should. I've even managed not to knock out that pestilent bastard, Icel, but I draw the line at serving Coelwulf as my lord.

He chose to leave Kingsholm. He abandoned his brother when he needed him, and I'll abandon him in turn.

Beyond the walls of the stables, no one stirs. I would hear them if they were about some task. But, I've purposefully woken early, and I'll make my escape before anyone can stop me. Old Cenred is on guard duty tonight. He won't even raise an eyebrow at my passage outside. How often has Coenwulf sent me on strange errands, at all times of the day and night? I'll use that to my advantage, even as I curse Coenwulf for dying and leaving me without his support as my lord and friend.

I'll find the fuckers that killed him. That deprived me of my lord and friend. Only then will I be able to rest. I should have taken them all, there and then, but Icel insisted on bringing Coenwulf back to Kingsholm. I shouldn't have listened to his words. I shouldn't have been persuaded.

Jethson nuzzles me, and I push his inquisitive nose aside.

"Not now, boy. There'll be time for that in the future."

My horse is a stubborn beast. I've been forced to move him far from Coelwulf's horse's stall, or they'd be no sleep for anyone inside Kingsholm. I take some perverse pleasure in knowing my horse hates Coelwulf's horse, Haden, just as much as I despise Haden's rider.

I watched Coelwulf, the evening before, as he sat beside his Aunt beneath the eagle-headed shields of Mercia and attempted to look as though he knew what he was doing. The bloody arse. I've never seen a man look more uncomfortable. It does bring me some small pleasure that Coelwulf wants this even less than I want him to have it. But it doesn't stop him from having it, and therefore, this is my choice to make.

I lead Jethson towards the open doorway, aware his hooves will make some noise but unable to do anything about that. I must hope that even if someone hears him, they'll merely think it's one of the horses in their stalls, restless after their enforced captivity for the last month. Maybe they'll even think it's Dever, pining for his master, dead and turning to ash even as I think it.

Outside, the moon is bright—a good time to leave the complex. I'll be able to make good time, get myself far from Kingsholm. And then I can begin my task of finding the bastard Raiders. How I hate them!

"Edmund." I sigh heavily. The words are barely above a whisper, coming from above me. Of all the people to see me, I don't want it to be Coelwulf. After all, he's the master at sneaking away undetected.

Footsteps on the wooden ladder, and I turn to meet his interested gaze. I expect to see anger on his face, his eyes flashing dangerously. I don't expect to see respect.

"Are you leaving because of me or because you need to avenge my brother's death?"

His words carry only the question, no outrage, no censure.

"Avenge your brother." I hate how easily he speaks of Coenwulf's death. Just saying the words makes my throat tight, and I have to blink away my sorrow.

"You shouldn't go alone. This is something we should all do, all of us, from Icel to Pybba, to Osmod and Cuthwalh. You're not the only man to lose a lord and friend. A brother."

I grimace. Coelwulf is right.

"Yet, you've not ordered the men to ride out?" I

spit the words at him. Coelwulf's eyes flicker now, flashing beneath the bright moonlight.

"I haven't told you to fucking not to?" he counters, eyes high into his blond hairline. He watches me intently. I don't want to break that look. I don't want to be the first to turn aside. And yet I am, all the same.

"That's really not the same thing," I divert.

"It really bloody is." Wulfred comments. I've not even realised he's behind me. I turn, gasp, on seeing Cuthbert, saddled and ready to ride out. He's not alone. Icel is there as well, glowering from atop Samson. Pybba stands beside Brimman, Beornberht and Athelstan, waiting with their mounts beside him. How have I not noticed so many horses missing from the stables

"What is this?" I demand, not at all surprised when that young scamp, Rudolf, knee-high to a grasshopper appears leading a surprisingly plaint Haden as well. That boy shouldn't be allowed anywhere near that bloody horse. I open my mouth to say as much; only then do I hear Rudolf's soft tones as he cajoles Haden.

"Good horsey. No need to go near that nasty beasty, Jethson."

I turn to Coelwulf, and a bark of laugher rips from my tight lips as I see the strain and fury on his face. It seems that Coelwulf has been unmanned by his horse's capitulation to the small child, Rudolf. Just one of the orphans to make Kingsholm their home.

"We're coming with you." Coelwulf tries to recover his poise, his voice too bluff, his eyes flashing towards where Rudolf strokes Haden's long nose.

"No, you're not. It's that shitting attitude that got us into this mess."

"So, my brother's death is a 'mess'?"

I'd not expected to hear such fury in Coelwulf's voice.

"Not at all. But, you're the ealdorman. You remain here, in Kingsholm."

"Fuck that," Coelwulf growls, while Icel nods in fierce agreement.

"So, we're going to go from having one ealdorman to another and still let him face the fucking Raiders." The words gush from my mouth as though a wound that can't be staunched.

It's Pybba who answers me.

"Being an ealdorman isn't enough. You bloody know that. We need our Lord to fight for us. And Coelwulf says he'll do that, so we'll let him. If he's shit at it, then we'll know not to do it again." Pybba's words, initially welcomed by Coelwulf, have quickly become less…. welcome. Again, a smirk plays around my lips. Coelwulf isn't appreciative of how well the men can read him.

"Fine. We'll all bloody go," I confirm, anger still touching my words. "But I'm leading this expedition, not you," I fling the words at Coelwulf. His face is already clouded by hearing Pybba's complaints. Mine only add to it.

I watch him. His eyes glance from Pybba to Icel to Edmund and even to Rudolf, who stands as severe as the other men. Tatberht meets Coelwulf's gaze evenly. He's prepared to see just what Coelwulf can do. Osmod and Ælfgar are less eager. But they're ready to ride to war beneath his instructions. And then my eyes turn on Hereman. If there's one man who should support me, it's him, but I know the bastard won't—bloody brothers.

"Our Lord will lead us," Hereman rumbles with his usual stubbornness. I seek my patience and find it lacking.

"We've not given our oaths to him, so he's not our fucking lord."

"Oh Edmund," Hereman grumbles at me. "Shut the fuck up. He leads us, or we stay here, and you'll be the next one of us dead, sliced and murdered by a Raider blade."

His words chill me, reminding me too easily of what happened to Coenwulf. Fuck. I loved that bastard. I loved him more than I do my bloody brother.

"I agree," Tatberht confirms.

"Me as well," Cuthwalh is the next to speak, and then all of the weak-willed fuckers start supporting one another. And as they do so, I watch a strange transformation take place in Coelwulf's stance. He might have given me respect for my actions, but he showed none for his own. Now, as the men, one after another, pledge that he is their leader, if not yet their oath lord, he stands taller. His broad shoulders settle, his head coming upright, meeting the eyes of those who speak for him.

"And me," Icel pronounces. His voice is as solid as a rock. I still think he has all the making of a lord, but he has no claim to any of it. Or so he says whenever he's plagued about it.

"Then we'll let our leader have the command," I unhappily announce. Jethson farts his disapproval, reaching across the divide as though to nip Haden. But beneath Rudolf's hands, the beast remains pliant, and now Jethson looks like a total arse.

"Thank you," Coelwulf speaks firmly. Has he really become a new man before my eyes? I remain to be convinced. And then he startles me.

"And now that's fucking solved, Edmund, you know where the attack took place and how to find the fucking Raiders. You can lead on."

I fix him with my eyes and know that he's still the cock he always was. He lifts one eyebrow at me as though to dare me to argue again. Fucking cock.

"Fucking follow me then," I growl, and the men line up behind me, all apart from Coelwulf, who stays at my side, having dismissed Rudolf with soft words of thanks which I don't want to hear. That boy is a bloody menace. All of six years of age and into everything and knowing everything about everyone inside Kingsholm. I don't want to believe that Coelwulf has any good in him. How can he after everything he's done?

Last night, lying beside Lady Cyneswith, Coelwulf's aunt, and my lover, I spoke my mind.

Her eyes were hard as she watched me in the flickering candlelight.

"Would you rather have no lord? Be sent from this place?" she demanded from me, her words angrier than her tone.

Of course, I'd tried to deny her words. The future she envisaged was bleak but not as bleak as my cold heart felt.

"Would you rather I had no one to protect me? No one to ensure Kingsholm remains the haven it is from the reaches of the ineffectual King Burgred of Mercia? The king would take Kingsholm in a heartbeat. It would eventually silence those who know that there is a claim to the kingship for my nephews, nephew," she'd corrected, a look of dismay on her face, "that is far stronger than anything Burgred can claim even though he's Mercia's king? For now." Her words had been ominous. Sometimes I forgot the power she could exert, the woman she was. She should have married a great lord, birthed fine sons, but she didn't. I suspect I know why, but I've never asked.

"No, but if he stays, then I can't."

"So, you would leave me as well?" Furious, she'd risen from the bed and flung a cloak around her naked shoulders. How I'd wanted to take back my words. But I could only be honest with myself and with her.

Her nephew would not be my lord.

She'd watched me, eyes ablaze. And I'd known then that I would leave her to save myself from Coelwulf even though I'd not wanted to. And now? Well, Coelwulf isn't yet my lord, and if I have my way, he won't survive our expedition to avenge Coenwulf. No, I'll allow the Raiders to kill him without a second thought, but not Coenwulf. Never Coenwulf, and yet they had done so.

We rode in silence. I brood as we make our way to Gloucester and the river crossing there. Coelwulf's silent at my side, his horse nickering unhappily whenever Jethson got too close to him. I determine not to notice how hard Coelwulf has to control his mount to stop him from surging ahead. What is this? Why is he trying so hard? Any man and beast can take directions from another. Why he chooses to do what he does is beyond me.

Together, the horses step onto the wooden bridge, the Severn surging below us. Jethson's ears flick at the unexpected noise of his hooves, but Haden, the daft bastard, does far worse than that. He stops having retraced the two steps he's taken. He plants all four of his hooves on the firm ground inside Gloucester and refuses to move, no matter what Coelwulf does.

I lead on, the rest of the men following me, and still, that damn horse stays behind. It seems that Haden might be my ally, even if Coelwulf isn't.

"Is he bloody coming?" Hereman grumbles, turning back to glance the way we've come. I don't follow suit. I know that horse isn't coming anytime soon. I'll get to avenge Coenwulf and do it without Coelwulf. That suits me just fine. And then? Well, then I can leave his service. I might risk losing the woman I love, but there are more women. There are always more women.

Tatberht and Eoppa stop as well, reining in their

horses and watching what isn't happening behind us.

I can't hear any hoof beats over the bridge, the unmistakable rumble of thunder that isn't thunder.

I grin for the first time since Coenwulf's death. I smile, and then I laugh, sounding too loud, almost hysterical.

"Fuck the bastard, come on, men, we'll get our revenge. We'll prove to that damn fool how it's done, and it's not with a horse that doesn't obey commands."

I don't know what I expect, but it isn't Icel's grin. The man is so grim; he never smiles.

And then I look to where he does.

"Bollocks," I explode, but Icel isn't alone in smirking. All of them are, Hereman chuckling so much I think he'll fall from his mount.

"There's always a way," Coelwulf calls as soon as he's in sight. He doesn't ride Haden. No, it looks as though he's stolen the pony used by the merchants, and now, his long legs drag along the wooden planks of the bridge, he rode across that bloody bridge, and fuck me, but Haden follows on behind, his eyes flashing blackly.

"There, you daft shit. You either do it, or I allow another to be my mount." As he speaks, Coelwulf dismounts, or rather, stands and the donkey carries on going. He reaches out, hooks the rein, and turns the pliant beast back towards Gloucester. One of the children has followed the donkey, and now she reaches for the reins and escorts the donkey back over the bridge. Haden comes to an immediate stop as soon as he's reached hard land again. No sooner has Coelwulf mounted than the brute skips to a gallop.

Now I'm laughing and for a different reason. Yes, there might well be a way of doing everything, but Coelwulf's far from the master of his mount.

"Come on, we need to keep up with him," Pybba calls, already urging Brimman onwards. Tatberht follows closely behind, and then the rest of the men until only Icel, and I remain.

I glance at him, expecting to see contempt on his face, but there's a tight smile there that I don't understand.

"He's a fucking liability," I reiterate.

"That he might be, Edmund. But he's our liability, and he'll make a good lord. In time."

"That remains to be seen," I glower. It seems to me that Coelwulf is winning the support of the men without even trying. I'm curious to see what will happen when he actually faces the Raider bastards. Then, I'm sure; he'll show his true nature – that of a weak-willed bastard who's scared of his own shadow.

I feel a slither of pity for my lover, but there's nothing I can do for her, not until she accepts that Coelwulf isn't ever going to fill the space left behind by her dead nephew.

On we rode. My mood sours the further we go from Gloucester. Ahead, Brimman has caught Haden, and now Coelwulf and Pybba ride together.

Of course, Pybba knows the way as well as any of us. This is our lord's land. We've ridden this way many, many times, but now we know that around the next bend of the river, there's a Raider camp, and we've come to kill them all.

No sooner have I thought it than I smell the smoke of their campfire—brazen bastards. I hurry to catch Coelwulf to determine his instructions and his means of killing them all, yet he doesn't stop. Haden, gathering his rear legs beneath him, galloping faster and faster, this time at the command of his rider, and I rein in tightly, a cry of warning on my lips.

"Come on, you sod," Icel calls over his shoulder, high in his saddle as Samson rides ever faster. "He means to show us what sort of lord he'll be, and I don't think you want to miss it."

"Miss it?' I muse. How can I miss it? More likely, I'll arrive in time to witness his failure. How can he expect to win without any form of plan in mind? He hasn't even scouted ahead. He doesn't know the way the camp's constructed. He doesn't know where the men will be.

A battle cry fills the air, and I smirk. Damn fucking fool, and slow Jethson even more. While the rest of the men stream onwards, I'm not taking the risk. Such a desperate attack won't wound my horse. Coelwulf's a damn fool and probably a dead one by now.

And then, I round the bend which shields the camp from view, and my mouth drops open, even as Jethson side-steps out the way.

Riding towards me, his face sheeted in maroon, his byrnie stained the deepest purple of blackberry's, Haden's nose no longer white and black but rather pink and black, comes Coelwulf. And not one of the fucking Raiders is still standing.

"And that," Icel says to me, a smirk playing around his usually tight lips. "Is how you win the hearts of your men and exact revenge for your brother's murder."

I swallow heavily. Unable to say anything to deny the truth of those words.

"Will you take me as your lord then, men?" Coelwulf calls, his voice deep and booming. He doesn't even look as though he's broken a sweat.

As one, Hereman, Tatberht, Eoppa, Ælfgar, Pybba, Cuthwalh, Eadfrith, Osmod, Cealwin, Athelstan and Beornberht leap from their horses' backs and kneel, one knee staying upright, head's bowed. Coelwulf's face is suddenly serious, his posture again rigid, his eyes glimmering with righteousness. "And you, Edmund, what of you?"

I feel Icel watching me as he dismounts more slowly to join the others. He dares me with that look to deny my new lord, and I'm tempted. I'm really fucking tempted. But I think of Coenwulf, of Lady Cyneswith, of what Coelwulf has accomplished without seeming to try, and I dismount as well, Jethson restless beneath me.

"Aye, My Lord Coelwulf. I think I fucking will."

PYBBA

AD865

Edmund has refused to come to Repton. I can't say that astounds me. He's never been one for pomp and ceremony. I still don't know what Lady Cyneswith sees in him, but what am I to say about that.

Now, I watch her just as carefully as I do my new lord, Coelwulf.

I like him. There's not much not to like about him. Yes, he's impetuous. Yes, he seems to make decisions with no more than a moment's notice. And yet? Well. I've not seen him make a wrong decision yet. Well, other than to let his aunt dress him for his presentation to the king.

Most would take this to be an admission that Coelwulf isn't yet the ealdorman of the Hwicce, but there's no one here who expects King Burgred to refuse his appointment to the ealdordom. If King Burgred were to do that, he'd lose one of his bastions that protects Mercia from the bloody Welsh of Gwynedd and Powys. He's not going to do that. I'm sure of it.

Still, Coelwulf looks uncomfortable. King Burgred sits at the front of the stone-built building, seeming not to notice Coelwulf, but I know men well enough to understand what he's doing.

The two men couldn't be more dissimilar. Coelwulf is tall, his long blond hair covering his shoulders. He has the stance of a warrior. Well, he has the bearing of a labourer, a ceorl, but he's also a warrior, and in time he'll grow thicker muscles than the ones he already claims.

Coelwulf wears a tunic rich with embroidery on the cuff and collar. The silvered emblem of his grandfather's once-held kingdom easy to detect with the eagle's hooked beak and sharp talons. What is Lady Cyneswith doing with such blatant and costly work on her nephew's tunic? She can't mean to proclaim his right to rule? Surely.

And yet. Well, I've known Lady Cynewith for many years. Her nephew for a matter of months. I'm not immune to what she sees on looking at him.

Coelwulf, for all he never thought to be an ealdorman, is more than an ealdorman. He's quick-witted, steadfast, fierce, violent and above all, loyal. Loyal to the ealdordom, he once left, only to return on the death of his brother. And I've witnessed a man who loves the people of the Hwicce, and not just the people who make Kingsholm their home. I admire him. Edmund doesn't. Well, he does, but in such a way that he'll never acknowledge.

"It's hot in here," Hereman huffs into my ears. He's not wrong. And he, just like Coelwulf, fiddles with his collar. I slap his hand aside, and he glowers at me. Some might fear violence breaking out right here, but for all Hereman's unpredictability, he can be relied on not to do that. For once.

"The women didn't go to all that trouble to see your dirty hands befoul the yellow of the tunic." At least in that regard, Lady Cyneswith has shown some wisdom. Had she dressed us in the maroon of Mercia's battle banner, complete with the eagle embroidery, then it would be impossible to ignore her intention. Actions speak far, far louder than words, and Lady Cynewith will have her intentions known, even if in such small, subtle ways.

Not, I think that the king's wife is foolish enough not to realise her game. I watch her face.

Lady Æthelswith might once have been a beautiful woman, but the years as Burgred's wife have aged her. Now, she sits wearing the finery of a queen; the daughter of a king, the sister of the kings of Wessex, and she seems to enjoy it as much as a slap of cold rainwater in her face. Her lips are twisted, her hands rigid on the wooden chair of state she sits within.

A young boy shuffles and fidgets at her side, but he's not her son. No, Beornwald is her nephew, and it seems she intends to have him proclaimed as her husband's heir.

My gaze passes from Coelwulf's back to Beornwald's face, and I know who I'd sooner was king of

Mercia. But of course, I'm merely a warrior, a member of Coelwulf's household troop. When it comes to the matter of kings, my opinion matters for nothing. Although, well, my opinion of who will be my lord does matter, if only to me.

"My Lord Coelwulf." King Burgred's voice is much softer than I expect it to be.

I watch as Coelwulf stands and then bows before his king. Burgred doesn't bid him rise, and that doesn't shock me. King Burgred has learned his tricks from his wife, and the Wessex woman is as devious as every other Wessex man or woman that I've ever met. They're about as loyal as a hound after a stag.

"You may rise," King Burgred eventually announces after I've taken at least fifty breaths. I'm impressed that Coelwulf has the demeanour to take such an outright afront. But then, Lady Cyneswith has been coaching her nephew ever since the summons came to attend the Easter Court of King Burgred held at the royal site and mausoleum of Repton. It's far from convenient. The Raiders might well be concerning themselves with the Wessex possession of Kent, but knowing how quickly the bastards can travel, it's not truly far enough away.

I itch to return to Kingsholm, and I'm not alone in that. And equally, that is why Edmund has been allowed to stay away from Repton. Kingsholm and its responsibilities must be protected. At all costs.

"I was sorry to hear of the death of your brother." Coelwulf's shoulders tense at this admission by the king. I can see all this quite easily, but consider whether it's just because I know Coelwulf slightly better than the king.

"The Raiders who brought about his death have long been forever sleeping," Coelwulf's words are meant softly, but he has the voice and command of a warrior leading his troops. Against the sound of Burgred's soft condolences, the comparison between the two couldn't be any more unfavourable.

Hereman leaves off playing with his collar to smirk at me. He's a mad bastard. His eyes are alight with what he's witnessing. One of his hands strays to his empty weapons belt. Perhaps he would make Coelwulf a king of Mercia here and now. After all, Coelwulf's grandfather was king, as was his grandfather's brother. Why the family lost their control over Mercia is much debated. Certainly, and as far as I can see, it was not well done. Not for the first time, I consider what Mercia would be if Coelwulf's brother had been its king. Undoubtedly, he wouldn't have died on the edge of a Raider blade besmirched in filth. Or, perhaps, he would have done.

"Ah, yes, well, very good then." I can tell that Burgred tries to match his tone to Coelwulf's. It only makes the comparisons even more unfavourable.

The other ealdormen of Mercia await their part in these proceedings. They must, along with the king, confirm Coelwulf as an ealdorman. I consider whether they'll do so or not. These men aren't as weaselly as their king, but I can't see that they're the men that Coelwulf is becoming.

"And now, we must vote, I believe?" As he speaks, King Burgred looks into the distance. I don't know who he's trying to confirm his words with, probably one of the bishops or perhaps his cleric.

"First, My Lord King, someone must nominate him." The words are smug, the head that bobs up before me grey with age. So, it's Ealdorman Wulfstan who thinks to speak first. I grimace. I don't like the man. There's something about him that's particularly unsettling. He's an older man, a firm ally and favourite of King Burgred, his chin showing the hoariness of his age.

For a moment, King Burgred falters, unsure what to do. I see now why Mercia suffers, as it does, under his kingship.

"Yes, yes, a nomination."

"I nominate Coelwulf as ealdorman of the Hwicce." The words are quickly spoken, flowing from Beornheard, as he stands and bows before the king. Beornheard is an old ally of the ealdormen of the Hwicce. All the same, I'm relieved that Ealdorman Wulfstan's hastily thrown piece of administrative correctness is dealt with deftly.

"And I second," this comes from King Burgred himself, the words again forced. He fixes Ealdorman Wulfstan with an unreadable expression. Perhaps the two aren't allies. Foolish, but what can King Burgred do? Ealdorman Wulfstan is a tricky fellow. I would trust him about as far as I could throw him. So not very far.

"Then the vote? All those for?" King Burgred

moves quickly to this part of the proceedings. I'm unsurprised that the cries of 'aye,' are far from a ringing endorsement, but they carry it all the same.

"Then, I'll take your oath." And now one of the bishops does appear. I believe it's Bishop Eadberht, but I might be wrong. I know Bishop Wærferth of Worcester, not Eadberht of Lichfield. But, it only takes one to make an ealdorman.

And now I'm stunned into silence, and again, Hereman is distracted from his itching to watch what's happening.

The kingdom of Mercia is old and has its fair share of saints and holy relics, upon which Coelwulf could swear his oath. What I don't expect to see is this. The box the bone is laid within is rich beyond imagination, the long bone inside yellowed like old teeth. I grimace to think of touching such a thing, and yet Coelwulf holds out his hand easily enough.

The words of the oath are filled with all the menace of the battlefield. They thrum through the structure of the stone-built church at Repton, beneath which the remains of Mercia's kings are forever interred, those of King Æthelbald, King Wiglaf. And his grandson Wigstan, who also happened to have been Coelwulf's cousin, although the two never met.

"By the Lord, and these holy relics, I pledge to be loyal and true to Burgred, the first of his name and king of Mercia. I'll love all that he loves and hate all that he hates, in accordance with God's rights and my noble obligations. I'll never, willingly, intentionally, in word or deed, do anything hateful to him; on condition that he keep me as is our agreement, now I subject myself to him and take his service."

The effect of hearing Coelwulf say such words makes me shiver. Beside me, Hereman's huge mouth has dropped open, and I'd nudge him to shut it, but every person in that church seems to be under the same spell.

Well, all apart from one. Through the multitude of people, some sitting, the majority standing, I feel the heat of someone's eyes on me, and I meet the knowing gaze of Lady Cyneswith. She's dressed as finely as the king's wife. And now I understand why.

Coelwulf was never meant to be the ealdorman. That position was to be filled by his older brother. But Coenwulf is dead now. While Lady Cyneswith was deeply unhappy with what happened to Coenwulf, I've noticed a change in her recently. Not, I think, that Coelwulf has seen it himself. Or even Edmund. Some people truly walk around with their eyes closed.

I nod, just the once, and her lips quirk just enough to know that she's seen it.

And then the sound returns to the room, and Coelwulf stands and makes his way back to his seat. Now Mercia has a new ealdorman and perhaps, in good time, a new king as well.

The rest of the proceedings are long and tedious, little and nothing, complaints about taxation, about the Raiders; a call to arms that Mercia isn't safe while the Raiders are in Kent, but it's virtually ignored. For now.

I sense Hereman growing restless. I do as well, and then, finally, the witan comes to an end, and Coelwulf is the first to stride from the front of the church, after his king, and with his aunt rigid on his arm.

As he draws level with me, he meets my eyes, his eyebrows raise and only then does he speak.

"Let's get the," a pause because his aunt is beside him. "Hell out of here, and back to Kingsholm. God alone knows what Edmund has done in my absence."

But Lady Cyneswith stops, her lips pursed, and this time not with humour.

"First, dear nephew, we must pay our respects at the tomb of your cousin." Coelwulf shudders at the thought, and now Lady Cyneswith grins.

"What, my warrior nephew? Scared of the dead?"

"Of course not, it's just. Well, I never knew him, and it's morbid."

"Perhaps, but he was your cousin and my nephew, and it's been many years since I was here, and I don't intend on returning anytime soon." This, more than anything, convinces Coelwulf.

Around the pair of them, the remainder of Mercia's ealdormen, thegns, king-thegns and holy men and women part. It's as Coelwulf and his aunt are a stone in the river to be moved around, not through. Only then does Lady Cyneswith move aside.

"Wait here," Coelwulf informs Hereman and me. I'm pleased not to enter the crypt. I have no fear of the dead, but rather, the weight of this building pressing over my head is to be avoided.

Outside, a biting wind ruffles the water on the River Trent that seems to encircle Repton. There are some ships there; trading vessels no doubt bringing supplies from elsewhere for the feast that must follow the witan. The cries of the people on board the ships are brought to me with the wind. I walk aside, eager to be away from the swirling mass of people, wrapping my cloak more tightly around me so that it doesn't flap so forcefully.

Hereman lumbers at my side, and wary eyes watch the pair of us. With a slight sneer, I note that the other ealdormen and king's thegns don't seem to have warriors as their closest confidants, but rather clerics or serious-looking young men and women with the marks of green ink on their fingers when I catch sight of them.

"This place is wide open," Hereman offers me in what he must think is an undertone, but which isn't. A servant turns, startled, an ealdorman's wife all but squeals in shock not realising she stands so closely.

"The river," and Hereman points eastwards. "It leads to the Humber estuary. It's like a slice through the Mercian kingdom."

I look where he points. The river stretches away beneath the brightness of the early summer's day. It's been a dreary winter. The promise of warm weather to come is welcome. But I see precisely what Hereman means. He has a good eye for such detail. That astounds me.

"The Raiders are in Kent," I retort, unease, all the

same, making its way felt along my spine. I don't want to be the fool who ignores the threat of the Raiders.

"They have ships. They can be anywhere at a moment's notice, or so it seems," Hereman grumbles. Perhaps he's right to offer the caution.

I watch King Burgred as he moves amongst the attendees of the witan. Despite the weight of ceremonial clothing that cloaks him, he's not an inspiring figure. I don't know if I'd ride to my death in his name. Yes, I would do so for the ancient kingdom of the Hwicce, over which Coelwulf is now named ealdorman. But would I do it for the rest of Mercia?

I examine Ealdorman Wulfstan. Him, I don't like and don't trust. There are rumours about him. He'll take the coin from anyone, for anything, provided they pay him well. They say his allegiance can be bought, that he'll petition the king on behalf of even the most ludicrous of requests, and that the king will accede to his demands. And with what Hereman says, I know a slice of fear. Ealdorman Wulfstan is lord over the lands through which the Trent flows towards the Humber. Ealdorman Wulfstan, should the Raiders turn their sights towards Mercia, might well be one of the first to encounter them. I feel my mouth twist with unease at that revelation.

And then Coelwulf returns, his aunt, white-faced at his side. He holds her steady by gripping tightly to her arm, and he shakes his head at my questioning look. Something has happened, but whether it's just being in the crypt, I don't know.

"Now, shall we get this," and he pauses while Hereman grins. We both know what he meant to say but didn't, because of his aunt. "Feast over and done with?"

"Yes," Lady Cyneswith announces. Her attention, just like Hereman's and mine, is on the people and surroundings. Coelwulf merely looks strained. He's not enjoying this. That doesn't amaze me. Coelwulf is the sort of man unfamiliar with the scrutiny of this type of gathering. His brother would have done better here. He would have shared a word with the other ealdormen and their wives. He would have known their names and where they rule in the name of their king. But would he have made a better impression? I doubt it.

"Come on," and Coelwulf's strained voice reflects his disquiet. I walk to his left, Lady Cyneswith between Coelwulf and me, while Hereman takes the right. Now, more and more gazes fall on us. I look down at the well-trodden path I'm walking, hiding a smile.

The men and women of King Burgred's court no doubt see what I see, what Lady Cyneswith sees, and what the people of Kingsholm have quickly realised as well. Lord Coelwulf doesn't want any of this, and that's precisely why he would be so bloody good at it.

I feel a soft touch on my arm, and see Lady Cyneswith watching me, her lips tight, one eyebrow high, belief in every fibre of her being. She knows it as well, and that'll be as much of a dangerous weapon as Coelwulf's blade itself.

RUDOLF

AD871

"**M**y Lord," I bow low before Coelwulf. My eyes are forced to travel higher and higher when I glance upwards. Coelwulf is a fierce warrior, but more than that, he's one of the tallest men I know. I eye the weapons belt around his waist, the seax hanging there with its double-headed eagle hilt, glittering even in the gloom, the eyes of the creature just bright enough to see, even from such a distance.

"You'll join my war band, as my squire," his words are filled with caution, and yet my heart leaps to hear them. This is all I've ever wanted.

"My Lord," I bow my head once more, having glimpsed his intense blue eyes but not wanting him to see how much his words make my heart soar.

"It won't be pleasant," he cautions. There's no humour in his voice. In fact, I believe he speaks reluctantly. Does he not want to bestow this honour upon me?

"My Lord," I keep my head level. I can't keep the wide grin from my slim cheeks. Why he does it, I don't care. All I know is that I want it.

"And you'll need to learn to meet my eyes," he glowers, his boots turning as he walks from before me. I hasten to follow, a flick of his right hand showing me I am to do just that. I'm not taken aback when he leads me towards the stables, with their low hanging roof and scent of fresh hay combined with horse manure, horse sweat, horse farts. Horse everything.

No doubt Haden has some requirement that needs my attention. How I love that horse, and how he adores me, and yet, even to his master, he's a truculent creature. I smirk at the thought of that as well. Haden and I have our secrets. We both keep them well.

"Here. You'll ride Dever when we travel, and so, he is now your horse, and you'll care for him alongside Haden."

Dever, as though knowing he's being spoken about, lifts his head from where he lies on the floor of the clean and tidy wooden stable, the hay fresh, the shit removed earlier that day and hauled onto the kitchen garden, slumbering beneath the whiteness of the winter snow.

"A horse, My Lord?"

"Yes, a horse. How else will you be my squire when I'm travelling, as I must do so much of the time. You'll ride Dever. In the heart of the rest of my warriors. You'll keep him safe and will be available to me whenever I need you. In return, I'll ensure you're taught how to use your blade, spear and axe and how to avoid a fight in the first place."

"My Lord," I demure, unsure what else to say. Certainly, I refuse to tell him how thrilled I am to be promoted to the position of his squire. It brings with it the promise that one day when I'm taller and broader, I'll be allowed to join his war band properly. That one day, I'll be a member of Coelwulf's war band.

"And you must learn to say more than just 'My Lord.' I've never heard you say so few words." His voice is pensive, and I hunt for the humour that I know is so often to be found there. Ealdorman Coelwulf is a brutal taskmaster and yet beloved all the more for that. He expects nothing from his men that he won't do himself. Only that morning, I found him shovelling out two of the horses' stables because it needed to be done, and Edmund had taken to his bed, nose streaming, unable to speak because his throat was so sore. I consider whether his aunt forced him to carry out the task, but I know that's not the case. Coelwulf wasn't always a lord. Rumour has it that he was once little more than a farm labourer, paid to do what small jobs were available.

"I won't let you down," I enthuse, looking from Dever to Coelwulf. A horse, and what an animal.

"The thing is, Rudolf, if you let me down, you'll probably be dead." The words sound callous, and yet they're not. He washes me with his fierce gaze as though weighing whether I understand them or not

Mercia is in turmoil. The Raiders are prevalent. They scour the land like snakes, hiding in the thick grasses, and her king is weak. Even I know that, and I'm little more than an orphan boy. I've been lucky enough to live within Kingsholm for all of my short life. Now, it seems, I'm to leave the safety behind Kingsholm's walls and venture where my lord does. And it won't be safe. And there will be no assurance that I'll return after every journey.

"Aye, My Lord. I do have ears to listen with."

"Hum," he growls. "And sometimes it seems to me as though every part of your body is listening to conversations it shouldn't be." I grin at his sharp tone. Some might think I should be embarrassed to have been caught eavesdropping when I shouldn't, but how else is someone such as I to know what's happening? I have no mother or father to tell me. And, I can fit into spaces that others can't, and so I can listen, and I do.

Knowledge has become my particular skill.

"You'll soon learn that life on the road gives few opportunities for smirking like that."

"Aye, My Lord," I offer. I know it's not the truth. The men who ride with Coelwulf are a breed apart. They find humour in even the harshest places, the most painful of injuries, and the deepest grief.

"He's a slow horse," Coelwulf continues, as though determined to ensure I know his decision is no real advancement for me. "You'll have to ensure he keeps up."

"Aye, My Lord. I'll soon have Dever reacting to my commands."

"I'm sure you will," Coelwulf responds, his voice, despite all he's said to the contrary, warm with humour as he turns to run his hand along Dever's curious black and white-nose.

And then he's gone, and Dever is standing, watching me as though he heard and understood every word spoken. Dever and I are hardly strangers to one another.

"Hello lad," I offer him. He hangs his head over the stable door, waiting for my extended hand to rub along his long nose to replace the warmth of Coelwulf's touch. He's a fine horse, a little older than some, I don't deny, but he was once a lord's horse. He's done well throughout his long life. I won't be forgetting that, even if it seems Coelwulf has misremembered that Dever was once his brother's steed.

I open the stable door and venture inside, Dever butting at me with a warm greeting, his warm hay-filled breath mingling with mine. He doesn't try to force me from my feet as other horses, such as the feisty Jethson might do.

"It seems we are to become great friends," I advise him. Those words don't seem to upset him. "And so, you might have to learn to gallop a little faster, canter at the speed of the rest of the horses." Now, I hear a chuckle, but not an unpleasant one.

Pybba pokes his head over the stable door.

"I wish you luck with that," he informs me, without malice. Pybba is older than Coelwulf, and he has wisdom that I think Coelwulf lacks. Or perhaps it's just that he doesn't need to make such quick decisions.

"He'll do as I say, I'm sure of it." My voice is filled with confidence and pride.

"It doesn't come down to that," Pybba retorts. "It's whether he's capable."

"Oh, he's capable," I confirm, nodding my head. "I know what he is and what he isn't."

"What he is, is an old horse, already into his twenties. Many horses don't live that long."

"And many do." While I appreciate Pybba's caution to me, I won't allow him to take this moment from me.

"He is a fine horse," Pybba changes tact. "Treat him well, and watch his front left leg. He injured it many years ago, and in the cold weather, it pains him or at least makes him limp." Pybba frowns as he speaks.

I nod eagerly now. "Thank you," I offer.

"Aye, lad, and when you're ready, I'll take you for your first lesson with a blade. Coelwulf knows I'm the man to begin your training. He fears he'll be too fierce with you."

"You'll train me?"

"I will, yes. I'm not so old as Cenred and the others who do nothing but warm their arses by the hearth and speak of days gone by when summers lasted forever, and winters were no inconvenience." I grimace at his word, and Pybba grins. As he does so, the years fall back from his lined face.

"I'm ready now," I announce, a lingering hand running along Dever's flank. I want to check his hoof, but I know he's well. He was yesterday.

"Then come. Bring your blade with you, and we'll see what you know."

Hastily, I say goodbye to Dever. He kicks the stable door, and I turn, startled.

"An apple," Pybba suggests, handing me a small, wizened old thing from this year's harvest as though he knew what would happen.

Dever takes the offered treat delicately, lifting back his black and white lips to reveal his huge yellowed teeth. He's dainty as he takes the treat from my open hand.

As he chews, I rub his nose once more. The black and white of his coat seems to run in canted lines so that one of his eyes shows clearly against the white, his other one, shadowed by the black.

After he's finished, he moves backwards, settling once more, and I can move aside. Pybba waits patiently for me. As we pass the next stall, he rubs his hand over Brimman's white-nose and then offers him an apple as well. I can see how Pybba keeps his horse as his ally. I'll have to learn to do the same with Dever. Haden is already my great friend. But our friendship isn't based on treats and trickery. No, we just appreciate one another's company.

We don't exit the sizeable stable building, but instead, Pybba walks to a space created by two of the stables being converted into one. It's not the largest space, but better than venturing outside where the snow lies deeply on the ground and only gets deeper and deeper with each gentle fall. It's bitterly cold out there, the smell of the wood fires from the lord's hall and other dwellings reaching my nostrils, enticing me with their warmth. But I know I'll be warm soon enough.

"Show me how you hold your blade?"

I have a small seax, the handle fits my hand easily, but it's about as sharp as cheese. I've spent much time scraping away the rust and revealing the shimmering blade beneath it, but nothing I do makes it sharper.

"Good," Pybba stands behind me, and I can feel his breath on my exposed neck as I hold the blade in front of me. "Good, not too tightly, but tight enough that you won't drop it if someone hits it."

He moves in front of me now, reaching for a blade that's been left on top of two bales of hay waiting for the horses.

"I hold my blade the same, but in a battle, be wary of your thumb. Sometimes it helps to curl it with your fingers."

I try the unfamiliar position, and I don't like it. I like it even less when Pybba thrusts towards me with his borrowed seax, and I drop my blade to the floor, the vibration unpleasant along my arm, so that I shake it from side to side.

He smiles without malice.

"That's what the man who taught me did to me. It seems only fair to continue the tradition." He shrugs a shoulder, amusement alive on his face.

I retrieve my seax from the floor, wishing I'd not fallen prey to such a tactic. This time I hold the blade with my usual grip. Pybba notes it but says nothing about it. I like that he doesn't berate me for ignoring his instructions.

"Now, much of fighting is to do with watching your enemy. See what they mean to do. You can tell by where they look and how they hold their weapon. And then you respond." With that, he jabs toward me, and I move my seax to counter his strike. Again, the blades colliding is painful, but I keep hold of the weapon this time.

"Good. But I made that easy for you." Again, there's no condescension in his words. I like that as well.

And so Pybba continues. Jabbing and turning so that I'm never really sure where he might attack from until some small tell gives it away. By the time he draws aside, I'm breathing heavily, and Pybba is barely sweating in the cold air.

"He's going easy on you." A voice rumbles, and Icel moves into view. I hadn't even realised we were being observed.

If I thought Coelwulf was a tall man, Icel is even taller. Some might consider him a giant. He must have once had thick dark hair, but now it's silver and shows no sign of disappearing, unlike most men even half his age. He has a spattering of hair on his chin and cheeks but no full beard. Not at the moment. I know full well that during the summer months, when Coelwulf's warband is hardly to be found at Kingsholm, Icel will allow his beard and moustache to grow out. He can't be bothered with shaving when there's no hot water to be found. And, as I've heard him say, shaving gives him something to do to fill the tedious days while winter rages outside the walls of Kingsholm.

"It's his first lesson," Pybba admonishes the older man. I stand taller, even though I want to sag to the floor with exhaustion. Icel has that effect on people.

"Well, a first lesson doesn't have to be quite so tame." For a terrible moment, I fear that Icel might take out his seax and continue the lesson. "In the reign of King Wiglaf, I first took a seax to the neck of my enemy." Icel's words rumble with menace.

"And that was your first lesson?" Pybba admonishes Icel. I'm amazed he'd do such a thing. Icel is a man of few words but many, many actions. He knows everyone within Kingsholm, better even than Lord Coelwulf.

"Perhaps not," Icel confirms, a rare smile playing around his thick lips. "When you believe Rudolf is ready, send him to me, and I'll teach him how to truly fight."

Pybba shakes his head, but it's good-natured.

"Why, because I've never truly fought Mercia's enemy?"

"No, because I have words to share with him which you will not."

With that, Icel walks away, and I watch him as he goes to hang his head over Samson's stable. I don't hear what passes between the two of them. I don't rightly believe I've ever been spoken to by Icel before, but the men are respectful of him, Coelwulf as well.

"Well done," Pybba says, a smile on his lips as he flexes his seax hand to ease some pain in it, I suspect. "Tomorrow, we'll do more, and every day until you can be left alone with Icel for his 'words', and then you can train with the rest of the warband."

My mouth drops open in shock at the statement. Somehow, I've not realised that this position as Coelwulf's squire means I am now a member of his war band to all intents and purposes. I'll not be equal with Hereman or Athelstan or even Tatberht, Ælfgar and Cealwin, older men like Icel, but I'll begin the process.

"Aye lad, and then one day, not only will you train with them, but you'll fight beside them in the shield wall, against Mercia's enemies; the Raiders, and mayhap Wessex as well." Pybba's face darkens as he speaks. I know of Mercia's enemy. I've heard the warriors discuss the men they kill, the battles they've fought in, the Mercians who don't ride back from such wars. But Wessex? Well, Wessex should be an ally, but even I know they're not.

"Will you teach me to fight with more than just a seax?" I ask. Although I should perhaps be terrified, I'm unashamedly not.

"I'll teach you to fight with every blade and with your fists, your feet, your forehead, your elbow and your body," Pybba promises me. "And when that's done, even Dever might have a few tricks to show you. I've not forgotten he was once Lord Coenwulf's horse. Coelwulf does you a great honour in giving you his brother's horse. I know you might think he's forgotten or that Dever is old and slower than the other horses, but he was good enough for the ealdorman of Kingsholm, and he'll be more than good enough for a young squire."

I nod. I can hardly take in all that's happened to me. I glance down at my boots, noting where the leather has worn smooth near the toes. I can also feel where my tunic is too short for me, almost reaching my elbows and not my wrists. And my trews? Well, they've been stitched more times than I care to remember. So many in fact, that Lady Cyneswith bid me learn to repair them myself.

"You'll have new clothes, and boots, and a warm cloak as well, if not two. Your lord will take care of you, and in return, you'll swear an oath to him when you do become a warrior."

"And how long will that take?" I'm already eager to ride beside the rest of the warriors, to take my place beside Coelwulf.

"About three years, if you're lucky." And just like that, all my pleasure disappears.

"Three years?" I cry. "I'm sure I'll be able to do it quicker than that."

"Aye lad, I imagine you are, but trust me, three years will come around soon enough. For now, practise what I showed you, and tend to Dever and Haden as you should. That is the beginning for every good warrior. Learning to care for those around him even while they learn the skills of killing."

I nod, chewing my lip as I do so.

"Tell me, why has Lord Coelwulf chosen me of all the boys in Kingsholm."

Now Pybba pauses and fixes me with an impressed smirk.

"If you've already noticed that, then there's hope for you yet, Rudolf." He leaves me, and I'm none the wiser. I think the lack of knowledge will bedevil me.

"Rudolf." I hear my name being called by Lord Coelwulf, and I rush through the sludgy snow and into my lord's hall. It seems that more than just my warrior's training has begun.

The story which follows, A Meeting of Equals, is the short story I wrote that gave me the character of Coelwulf and some of his warriors, as well as Coelwulf's feelings towards King Alfred of Wessex. This story is available on the Aspects of History website to read for free, but I thought it might be fun to include it here. Just so you can see how it's all developed since then.

In The Last King books, as they stand, Coelwulf hasn't yet met Alfred. But it's coming. Soon.

A MEETING OF EQUALS?

I 'm used to dealing with warriors. I'm not sure what to make of the man before me. I've heard a great deal about King Alfred. It seems much of it is true. I confess I'm disappointed.

I came here to find an ally in arms, prepared to assist me in beating back the Viking Raiders, a man committed to keeping his kingdom whole, as I endeavour to do with Mercia.

Alfred is not a warrior. Far from it. His hair might once have been blond, but is now some indeterminate shade of blond and grey. I thought him a young man, well, younger than I at least. I suppose that doesn't necessarily make him young. How strange it is to see those who are younger than me seem aged.

His eyes flash dull blue, and some wisps on his cheeks and above his lips, attest to the fact that he isn't capable of growing a full beard. Lucky bastard.

But more than anything, it's his lack of muscles that tell me the truth of who this man is. How, I think, has he fought the Vikings for all these years?

We meet as equals, that gives me some hope. He doesn't expect me to bow before him. Instead, he walks to greet me, hand outstretched to clasp my forearm. I mirror the movement. This is altogether far too fucking civilised.

"Lord Coelwulf," a smile tightens his lips, and his voice is deeper than I suspected it would be as I lightly grasp his forearm, feeling less muscle than I'm used to encountering.

"King Alfred," I use his title. I know he's been crowned. I know he's been chosen by Almighty God to rule Wessex. I refuse to insist on such pretensions and often refuse to respond to 'lord,' most notably when it's Edmund or Icel who try and insist on the formality. It depends on how difficult I'm feeling.

We pause then, two kings, for I have also endured the tedium of a holy coronation ceremony, each eyeing up the other. I consider what he sees when he looks at me. We couldn't be more different if we tried.

I tower over him, able to see his growing bald spot easily. My arms could crush him if he were my enemy. My beard is as light as the day, my long hair reaching beyond my shoulders, no hint of grey, or even white to be seen. My skin is shaded a permanent warm shade. I spend all of my time outdoors. It's almost impossible to get me beneath the shadow of a roof, apart from during the winter months, when there's no choice but to seek shelter from the extreme weather.

And that's not the only difference. I'm dressed as a warrior, the only jewellery I condescend to wear is a symbol of my claim to Mercia, the two-headed eagle broach, an ancient family heirloom. My true claim is the sword I carry, crowned with the self-same symbol. It marks me for who I am and what I stand for. I am Mercia.

While King Alfred doesn't wear his crown, he's a man of a civilised court. His tunic seems dipped in molten gold, his neck adorned with a golden cross, and he even has clean shoes! It's the final point that makes my eyebrows furrow. I can't remember the last time I had clean shoes. Hiltiberht has more important things to worry about than whether my boots are muddy or not. He must care for my mount, Haden, and see to his needs, which are many and varied and likely to change on a day to day basis. That horse is a monster of changeability.

I almost smirk at the thought of him, kicking the stable doors, even as I left him.

But, I confess, despite my apparent advantages over King Alfred of Wessex, I feel uncomfortable.

While I both respect and hate my Viking enemy, I feel I have the upper-hand when forced into tedious exchanges with them. I expected to feel the same here, but I'm not sure that I do.

A long silence stretches between us. What happens now? Usually, a diatribe of abusive language would pass between the two sides. I'm not entirely sure how to react to a man who not only wants to be my ally but is unarmed. I can't even see an eating dagger on his belt. This man is supremely confident, and yet, I believe he's weak.

I open my mouth and then close it. I've stepped back from our initial greeting, and now I feel as though I tower over him even more.

There's a strained expression on Alfred's face and I presume his courtly manners have deserted him. I never had any, so I feel better about that.

"Talk to me of your proposals," I find the words from somewhere.

This seems to recall him to our purpose.

"Of course," his deep voice, so at odds with his appearance, thrums with just those words. "Sit with me," he offers, turning to indicate the two chairs that have been set out for our meeting. When the request was made that we bring our chairs to this meeting of kings, I found it ludicrous.

But given Alfred's elaborate wooden chair, so heavy I imagine an ox, not a horse, was forced to bring it to our meeting place, it's taken altogether more planning than I've put into my stool. It's the one I use when I'm fighting Raiders and camping on some god-forsaken hill. And that's only when Hiltiberht remembers to pack it. I would be just as happy with the floor beneath my arse.

Here, Alfred wins the game of diplomacy. Or perhaps he doesn't. We might be on neutral ground, but this smacks a little of desperation. Alfred hopes to impress. But having a great big chair doesn't impress me. Not at all.

Neither would a pile of severed heads, although the Vikings would appreciate such a statement.

As I settle on my stool, our heads now level, I appreciate the subtleties that Alfred is trying to employ.

He must know what I look like, and my reputation speaks for itself. In place of that, he has nothing but a crown, or rather a chair, with which to taunt me.

"Your reputation as the man the Vikings are scared of interests me." I'm sure it does. I wait for him to say more, but when he merely waits, his hands resting in his lap, I realise he expects me to repay the compliment. I flounder. What can I say about him? He's survived, more by luck than skill. I've always thought derisively of that. Perhaps he deserves my respect. There's little about him to win the trust of others, to make them pledge their lives to him—nothing, other than his birthright and his tenacity. I wouldn't think it enough.

"Your reputation for survival interests me." I have no idea if I'm saying the correct thing. His facial tells are far from reassuring.

"The Vikings are rarely terrified of anyone," King Alfred states, ignoring my feeble efforts.

"They believe they're the most fearless warriors ever to live. They don't expect to encounter anyone who can beat them, and certainly not here. They believe our island is ripe for the taking."

"And we have shown them that's not the case." I think he tries to sound firm, assert that fact, but it sounds feeble, even with his deep voice.

"Individually, we've been effective, but together we could be much more." Alfred's eyes light up at the thought. I wish the idea of an alliance filled me with as much delight. I've been alone since King Burgred left Mercia, and it's not lost on me that much of that blame must lie with Alfred and Wessex. Burgred was his brother by marriage, and Alfred refused to assist him against the Vikings. Wessex has paid the price for that oversight. Mercia has as well.

"If we worked together, how would we reach decisions?" I'm used to deciding and having my warriors follow my commands without argument. I don't think that Alfred would do that. Neither do I believe his sour-faced warriors would agree to follow my instructions.

Alfred seems to consider my question carefully; his eyes narrowing in concentration.

"When King Burgred ruled Mercia, we had an alliance of mutual support," Alfred speaks slowly, perhaps worried he'll upset me. And he has. Only real strength of will prevents me from pointing how that arrangement was abandoned.

"But how were decisions reached about what constituted mutual support and what situations required reciprocal support?"

"Mercia was under almost constant attack both from the north and the east. Wessex did what it could for Mercia. Mercia never once came to the aid of Wessex." Alfred's tone has grown sharp, his blue eyes reflecting his anger, even though I've not accused him of anything.

"Mercia is still under attack." The fact I have to say this astounds me.

"Mercia still stands," is Alfred's immediate reply. I want to laugh. Why are we arguing about this? Does he think that Mercia still 'owes' him, and Wessex, something?

I sigh, running my hand through my hair. I didn't want to come here. I knew it would be a waste of time. I meet the eyes of Pybba. He nods at me, as though agreeing with my thoughts.

Pybba didn't want this meeting. Pybba was vocal about that, and Pybba is a wise man, the loss of his hand, a few years ago, fighting the Vikings, making him eager to kill as many as he can. He and young Rudolf are a fierce combined force. I've almost thought to pity the Vikings who come against them, thinking them weak; a slight youth and a one-handed warrior. They're soon proved wrong.

"Wessex still stands as well, and while I fight the Vikings, you seem to do little but beget children and make alliances with the Vikings."

There, I've said it. It brings me no joy, and I speak in a flat voice.

A murmur of conversation swells amongst those who watch us. It might only be Alfred and I who speak, but many more witness our discussion.

Do we argue about the future of our kingdoms, or is there something else at stake? I wish I knew.

I know war and battle, not politics. Violence has allowed me to hold onto Mercia. I'm unsure if that's the same for Alfred. If it is it's through battles fought in his name, not by him. I know men and women speak of his survival against the Vikings with awe, but what has he actually done, other than hiding and then rely on someone else to fight his battles for him?

He has not stood and fought, as I have. He has not lost close friends and allies. He has not fought men and women hungering for his death. He has not worn the blood of others as his crown. He has not been hunted by thousands of Vikings intent only on his death, as I have.

"You and I are more alike than different. We've both been forced to use compromise when we didn't want to. What matters is people's lives and livelihoods. How that's accomplished is of less importance." Alfred flutters his hands, dismissing my concerns. That boils me, and I can see Pybba growing frustrated with this man who thinks to use words as weapons, rather than weapons as words. I know what I would do.

"So you propose an alliance of mutual support where the prize is maintaining what we currently hold?"

I feel I have to force the issue.

"An alliance of mutual support where the prize is the knowledge that others will also fight for your kingdom if it's overrun."

I don't believe this is worth my time or consideration. The Mercians support me. Always. They will always take up arms to protect what belongs to them. They will not do that for the kingdom of Wessex. I know that.

Still, I'm curious.

"And how would we announce such? How would the people of Mercia and Wessex know of this accord, and know not to take up arms against one another?"

"A symbol of our alliance should suffice."

"What sort of symbol?"

And now Alfred's eyes cloud. Already, I don't trust him and his ambitions. I'm sure that the next word out of his mouth will be London. What is it with the Vikings and the kings of Wessex? They covert London above all else. I would much sooner have Gloucester, or Tamworth or even Northampton, but all they want is London and the stinking river that flows beside her.

"A coin."

"A what?" Of all the things he could have said, I would not have expected him to mutter those words.

"A coin," and he places an object into my hand.

I almost don't want to look, to drag my eyes away from his, trying to determine the truth behind such a simple demand, but the weight of it forces me to eye the object placed into my waiting hand.

It is a coin. I'm not entirely sure what's so special about it.

"A mark of unity," Alfred states, pointing to the surface of the object. Only then do I look closer, and then even closer.

Ah, I understand now.

"It's been done before, and now it would be a mark of our alliance against a common enemy," Alfred urges, and I'm aware that it has been done, and I'm also aware that doesn't mean it needs to be done again. Once was surely enough?

It seems that Alfred has tried an alliance with Mercia, by marrying a Mercian woman while his sister married the Mercian king, and now he devises a new ploy.

"King Berhtwulf of Mercia and King Æthelwulf of Wessex, together, on one coin." Alfred's voice is high with excitement, but I confess, his words fail to impress me. What use is a coin against the Vikings? What good will such a trinket gift to me? Will it replenish my lost numbers? Will it drive the Vikings from my lands?

Will it make my people yearn to fight for Wessex? Will it make the Wessex warriors keen to fight to protect Mercia? I can't see it.

What I do see causes a tight smile to touch my lips.

"Who will be first?" I ask, turning my gaze back to Alfred, enjoying the slip of his eager smile. He's like a child who thought to gain something by only mentioning half of what they wanted, in the hope that the other wouldn't appreciate what was being arranged. It's similar to giving away something you only desire a little to gain something you genuinely hunger.

King Berhtwulf was not my ancestor. He was one

of the kings who should never have ruled Mercia. I hardly think it fitting to wish to emulate him.

"First?" Alfred asks. "Each coin has two sides. There will be a side for Mercia and one for Wessex."

The thought should probably thrill me; only it doesn't. Such an alliance speaks not of equals, but of one having superior control over another. And Alfred isn't finished yet.

"They would be struck and distributed from London."

"But London is Mercian."

"London is Mercian, but it is the centre of England's trade. Those from far and wide, know of London's great wealth. Such coins will be used by traders from all over Frankia and the northern kingdoms. They'll spread the word that Mercia and Wessex are united. That Mercia and Wessex will defeat the Vikings."

I can't see that any of those events will come about. Why would traders speak of a simple coin? Coins are for buying and selling, not for proclaiming an alliance.

But my attention is caught by Pybba. He has heard every word Alfred has spoken, and I can see that he finds the proposition appealing. That surprises me. He was so against this meeting.

And really, what am I giving away?

This is not an alliance that offers anything other than a promise, and I know that such is far more potent than King Alfred truly understands. The hope of ridding the twin kingdoms of the Vikings will be beguiling, and enticing, I can almost appreciate just how King Alfred has stayed in control of his kingdom, even though his hands are softer than a child's. Has he ever killed a man? Does it even matter when he thinks such clear thoughts?

"I'll consider your suggestion." I sit back on my stool as I speak, only then realising just how far forward Alfred has been sitting, and how eagerly those in his entourage listen to his words.

Alfred needs this token far more than I do, that much is evident.

And really, what do I have to lose?

I would sooner he allied with me than with the Vikings.

I dredge a smile to my cheeks. It feels unfamiliar, and perhaps, it's a little daunting, because Alfred shudders back from my presence.

"I'll consider it carefully," I reiterate. I'm not about to agree straight away. Why would I? I'll make King Alfred sweat for a little longer yet.

CAST OF CHARACTERS

Coelwulf's household warriors
Coenwulf, Coelwulf's older brother
Coelwulf rides Haden
Edmund rides Jethson
Pybba rides Brimman
Rudolf rides Dever
Icel rides Samson
Hereman
Eoppa
Wulfred
Ælfgar
Tatberht
Cuthwalh
Eadfrith
Osmod
Cealwin
Athelstan
Beornberht

Bishop Wærferth of Worcester
Bishop Eadberht of Lichfield

Ealdorman Beornheard

Ealdorman Wulfstan

The royal family of Mercia

King Burgred of Mercia

     m. Lady Æthelswith in AD853 (the sister of King Alfred)

          they have no children

Beornwald – a fictional nephew for King Burgred

Places Mentioned

Gloucester, on the River Severn, in western Mercia.

Hereford, close to the border with Wales

Lichfield, an ancient diocese of Mercia. Now in Staffordshire.

Tamworth, an ancient capital of Mercia. Now in Staffordshire.

Repton, an ancient capital of Mercia. St Wystan's was a royal mausoleum.

Gwent, one of the Welsh kingdoms at this period.

River Severn, in the west of England

River Trent, runs through Staffordshire, Derbyshire, Nottingham and Lincolnshire and joins the Humber

Kingsholm, close to Gloucester, an ancient royal site

The Foss Way, ancient roadway running from Lincoln to Exeter

Watling Street, ancient roadway running from Chester to London

MEET THE AUTHOR

I'm an author of fantasy (viking age/dragon themed) and historical fiction (Early English, Vikings and the British Isles as a whole before the Norman Conquest, as well as two 20th century mysteries), born in the old Mercian kingdom at some point since AD1066. I like to write. You've been warned! Find me at https://linktr.ee/MJPorterauthor, mjporterauthor.com and @coloursofunison on twitter. I have a newsletter, which can be joined via my website.

Books by M J Porter (in chronological order, not publishing order)

<u>Gods and Kings Series (seventh century Britain)</u>
Pagan Warrior (audio book coming soon)
Pagan King
Warrior King

The Eagle of Mercia Chronicles (from Boldwood Books)
Son of Mercia
Wolf of Mercia

The Ninth Century
Coelwulf's Company – Tales from before The Last King
The Last King (audio book now available)
The Last Warrior (audio book coming soon)
The Last Horse
The Last Enemy
The Last Sword
The Last Shield
Book 7 (coming soon)

The Tenth Century
The Lady of Mercia's Daughter
A Conspiracy of Kings (the sequel to The Lady of Mercia's Daughter)
Kingmaker
The King's Daughter

Chronicles of the English (tenth century Britain)
Brunanburh
Of Kings and Half-Kings
The Second English King

The Mercian Brexit (can be read as a prequel to The First Queen of England)

The First Queen of England (The story of Lady Elfrida) (tenth century England)

The First Queen of England Part 2
The First Queen of England Part 3

<u>The King's Mother (The continuing story of Lady Elfrida)</u>
The Queen Dowager
Once A Queen

<u>The Earls of Mercia</u>
The Earl of Mercia's Father
The Danish King's Enemy
Swein: The Danish King (side story)
Northman Part 1
Northman Part 2
Cnut: The Conqueror (full length side story)
Wulfstan: An Anglo-Saxon Thegn (side story)
The King's Earl
The Earl of Mercia
The English Earl
The Earl's King
Viking King
The English King

Lady Estrid (a novel of eleventh century Denmark)

Fantasy

<u>The Dragon of Unison</u>
Hidden Dragon
Dragon Gone
Dragon Alone
Dragon Ally

Dragon Lost
Dragon Bond

<u>As JE Porter</u>
The Innkeeper

20th Century Mysteries

The Custard Corpses – a delicious 1940s mystery (audiobook now available)

The Automobile Assassinations (sequel to The Custard Corpses)

Cragside - a 1930s murder mystery

Printed in Great Britain
by Amazon